REY MYSTERIO

HIGH-FLYING LUCHADOR

by Lucia Raatma

Consultant:
Mike Johnson, Writer
PWInsider.com

CAPSTONE PRESS
a capstone imprint

Velocity is published by Capstone Press,
1710 Roe Crest Drive, North Mankato, Minnesota 56003.
www.capstonepub.com
Copyright © 2014 by Capstone Press, a Capstone imprint.

Library of Congress Cataloging-in-Publication Data
Raatma, Lucia.
Rey Mysterio : high-flying luchador / by Lucia Raatma.
pages cm. — (Pro wrestling stars.)
Includes bibliographical references and index.
Summary: "Describe the life and career of pro wrestler Rey Mysterio"—Provided by publisher.
ISBN 978-1-4296-9973-0 (library binding)
ISBN 978-1-4765-3583-8 (ebook pdf)
1. Rey Mysterio—Juvenile literature. 2. Wrestlers—United States—Biography—Juvenile literature. I. Title.
GV1196.R45R33 2014
796.812092—dc23 [B]   2013009486

Editorial Credits
Mandy Robbins, editor; Sarah Bennett, set designer; Heidi Thompson, book designer; Laura Manthe, production specialist

Photo Credits
Dreamstime: Outline205, 8-9; Getty Images: Alberto E. Rodriguez, 44, FilmMagic/Jill Ann Spaulding, 33 (inset), Frank Micelotta, 16, 39, Scott Barbour, 40, WireImage/Bob Levey, 27; Globe Photos: Milan Ryba, 36-37, Stan Gelberg, 10 (inset); iStockphotos: anthony myers, 26 (lucho), kevinruss, 6; Newscom: ABACAUSA.COM/Daniel Kramer, 4-5, NOTIMEX/ Guillermo Gonzalez, 22, Notimex/Guillermo Gonzalez, cover, WENN Photos/Carrie Devorah, 21, WENN Photos/David Mepham, 13, ZUMA Press/Matt Roberts, 31, ZUMA Press/ Panoramic, 35, ZUMA Press/Z Sports Images, 28-29; Photo by Wrealano@aol.com, 9, 15, 43 (both); Shutterstock: Africa Studio, 25 (food), apartment, 17, Barbra Ford, 42 (rings), Dan Kosmayer, 10 (TV), Dancestrokes, 7 (inset), dubassy, 19, dwori, 25 (barbells), Gemenacom, 7 (map), ktsdesign, 14, Late Night Rabbit, 42 (rattle), Mayboroda, 26 (rosary), Mike Flippo, 32-33 (piñata), OlegDoroshin, 24-25 (background), Potapov Alexander, 11 (lizard), SerialCoder, 41, StudioSmart, 43 (teddy bear), Zubada, 11 (hummingbird); U.S. Army photo by Spc. Eric Martinez, 45; Wikimedia: Fatima, cover, 1 (background), felipe bascunan, 24

Artistic Effects
Shutterstock

Printed in the United States of America in Stevens Point, Wisconsin.
072013   007589R

TABLE OF CONTENTS

INTRODUCTION:

A HIGH-FLYING PERFORMER

He may be small, but Rey Mysterio has a huge presence in the pro wrestling world. With his flashy masks and high-flying style, he makes a big splash in the ring.

Rey Mysterio shot to fame in the 1990s. At that time he was competing in World Championship Wrestling (WCW) in the United States. He eventually made a name for himself in World Wrestling Entertainment (WWE). In 2006 Rey became the lightest World Heavyweight Champion in WWE history. In the years since, he has experienced many challenges and successes as a wrestler.

For Rey Mysterio, there are always new moves to try and ways to keep his wrestling fresh. He explained it this way in the book *Rey Mysterio: Behind the Mask.*

"After all these years, you'd think I'd have worn out the possibilities. But the opposite is true. I feel as if I have a lot more left to explore. I have a long list of moves I haven't found the right moment to reveal. The partner, the event, the time, have yet to come."

REY MYSTERIO'S STATS

REAL NAME
Oscar Gutiérrez

HEIGHT
5 feet, 6 inches (168 centimeters)

WEIGHT
175 pounds (79 kilograms)

SIGNATURE MOVES
Dropping da Dime, West Coast Pop, Frog Splash, 619

CHAPTER 1:
GROWING UP IN TWO WORLDS

Rey Mysterio was born Oscar Gutiérrez on December 11, 1974, in Chula Vista, California. This city is in southern California near San Diego. It is very close to the Mexican border.

When he was growing up, young Oscar and his family lived in San Diego. The family did not have a lot of money. Oscar's father, Roberto, worked in a warehouse in Tijuana, Mexico, but he wanted his family to live in the United States. So every day, Roberto traveled from San Diego to Tijuana to work. He would leave early in the morning and come home late at night. Oscar's mother, Maria del Rosario, worked as a housekeeper.

Oscar had an uncle named Miguel Ángel López Díaz, who also lived with Oscar's family. Díaz was a construction worker during the day. But on Friday nights, he was a **luchador**. His ring name was Rey Misterio. Díaz performed in Tijuana, and Oscar would often go and watch. He loved spending time with his uncle and meeting the other wrestlers.

TIJUANA

luchador—a Spanish term for a professional wrestler in Mexico

Mount
Whitney

Las Vega

kersfield

SAN DIEGO

NI

a

GELES
Beach

an Ana

3506

San Diego

Tijuana Mexicali

LEARNING FROM UNCLE REY

Oscar looked up to his uncle and wanted to become a professional wrestler too. At age 8, Oscar began training with his uncle. Even though he was young, he proved that he was tough. Sometimes he did as many as 500 push-ups in one workout.

The gym where Oscar trained was not fancy. The ceiling leaked, and the mat was old and worn-out. But the men and boys who worked out there didn't worry about what the gym looked like. They were committed to becoming strong and skilled in the wrestling ring.

WHAT IS LUCHA LIBRE?

Lucha libre is a Mexican style of high-flying pro wrestling. Stars of lucha libre have to be very athletic and strong. Many of the wrestlers wear masks. In fact, it is rare to see lucha libre wrestlers without their masks on.

In lucha libre, smaller wrestlers in the flyweight and cruiserweight classes often compete against bigger wrestlers in the heavyweight division.

As part of the performance, there are two types of wrestlers in lucha libre: those who act as heroes and those who act as villains. A hero is known as a **babyface** in the United States, and a cientifico or técnico in Mexico. A villain is known as a **heel** in the United States and a rudo in Mexico.

babyface—a wrestler who acts as a hero in the ring

heel—a wrestler who acts as a villain in the ring

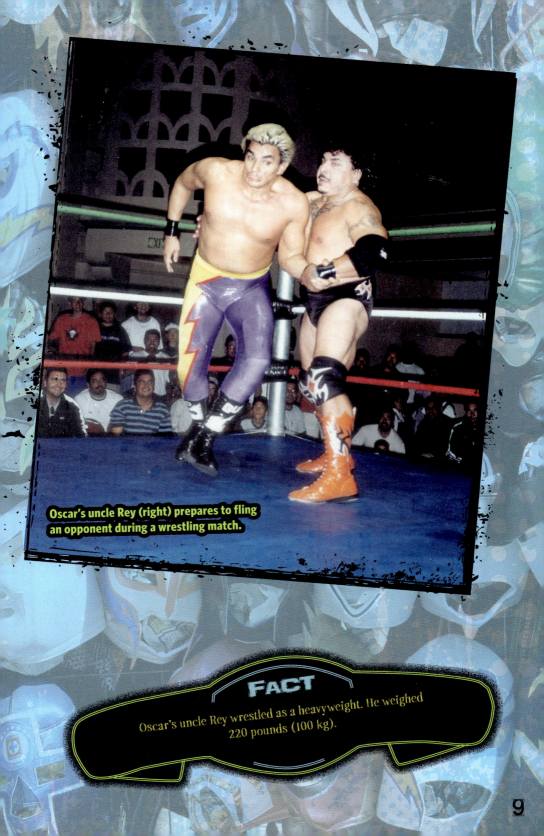

Oscar's uncle Rey (right) prepares to fling an opponent during a wrestling match.

FACT

Oscar's uncle Rey wrestled as a heavyweight. He weighed 220 pounds (100 kg).

CHAPTER 2:
ROAD TO SUCCESS

Oscar's teenage years were a very busy time for him. His family had moved to Tijuana, but he still went to school in Chula Vista, California. Most days, his mother would drive him to school. But if the traffic was heavy, he would walk several miles to school. In addition to working hard at school, Oscar had chores at home. He cooked meals and washed his own clothes. On top of it all, Oscar also worked at a pizza restaurant. While he worked he often caught glimpses of pro wrestling on the restaurant's TV. He saw stars such as Hulk Hogan, Tito Santana, and Ricky Steamboat in action.

Hulk Hogan (left) and Ric Flair (right) were popular pro wrestlers when Oscar was growing up.

training

test

Oscar had many responsibilities to juggle, but he wanted to wrestle more than anything. To be a wrestler in Mexico, though, he had to take a special test to be licensed. The test was hard—four or five hours long. It covered basic conditioning and wrestling skills. Oscar's uncle wasn't sure he was ready, but eventually he let Oscar take the test. He passed!

Oscar wanted to be known as Rey Misterio Jr. But Uncle Rey thought his nephew needed more experience before he earned that name. Oscar's uncle gave him his first wrestling name—the Green Lizard. Oscar hated it. He begged his uncle to give him a new name. Eventually, he got one. Oscar's new wrestling name was Colibri, which is Spanish for "hummingbird." As Colibri, Oscar wore a bright-colored costume. And he proved to be as quick and energetic as the bird he was named for. Soon Colibri had fans all over Mexico.

COLIBRI

the Green Lizard

FACT

In Spanish "The Green Lizard" is *La Lagartija Verde.*

TAKING ON A WHALE

Even though Oscar had a growing group of fans, many wrestling promoters would not schedule him. They were worried that he was too small and that he might get hurt. Oscar continued to train and tried to put on weight.

Finally, a promoter named Benjamin Mora agreed to book Colibri in a big arena matchup. It was against Shamu, a wrestler named for a famous killer whale. Shamu wasn't taller than Colibri, but he was certainly heavier.

The match started slow, with Colibri and Shamu locking up a few times. Colibri wasn't used to the size of the ring. It was bigger than the ring he had trained in. He had to get away from the ropes, where he and Shamu kept locking up. Colibri performed a dropkick and got some applause.

"I was very, very nervous. The knots in my stomach got tighter as I walked out of the locker room dressed as Colibri. Some kids near the runway pressed close to high-five me. I started slapping their hands back. I was acting cool, but my stomach was churning all over the place." —**Rey Mysterio on what it felt like before entering the ring to face Shamu** (Rey Mysterio: Behind the Mask)

Colibri flipped backward from the top of the ropes and slammed into Shamu. That earned him more applause, and his confidence grew. He finished the match by jumping up, hooking Shamu, and finishing him off with a move called a Frankensteiner. The crowd cheered, "Bella lucha! Bella lucha!" That means "good match," and it was.

SHAMU'S STATS

HEIGHT
5 ft, 4 in (163 cm)

WEIGHT
220 lbs (100 kg)

POPCORN
MATCHES

Before long, Oscar started getting booked in more matches. He traveled to the nearby towns of Mexicali and Tecate. But his home base was still Tijuana Auditorium, which was right next to his gym.

Colibri's earlier matches were called popcorn matches. The big name luchadors would wrestle later in the evening, but Colibri was scheduled earlier. People would come early, order popcorn, and settle in to wait for the later matches. But Colibri surprised the audiences with his style and acrobatic moves. As Colibri became better known, more people came early to watch him.

It was at these popcorn shows that Colibri started inventing his moves. He'd take someone else's move and add a twist to it. He'd add a flip or he'd jump higher. The crowd cheered. Colibri fed off their excitement.

Oscar graduated from popcorn shows to being the first match in the regular schedule. Then he graduated to the second match, which was a big move.

FACT

In his first year of professional wrestling, Oscar was named Rookie of the Year by the Mexican Wrestling Commission.

BECOMING
REY MYSTERIO

For years, young Oscar had wanted to be called Rey Misterio Jr., in honor of his uncle. But Uncle Rey didn't want to rush it. So Oscar kept competing as Colibri and slowly earned the respect of other wrestlers, including his uncle.

One night, he had a **tag team** match. Oscar was paired with Thunderbird. They were competing against Shamu and his partner Gatonico. But before the match started, the announcer said something important was about to take place.

Oscar had no idea what was about to happen next. But suddenly Uncle Rey appeared with a new mask for Oscar. He told the audience that Colibri was his nephew, and his name was about to change. Going forward he would be called Rey Misterio Jr. Young Oscar was overwhelmed by the honor. Tears ran down his cheeks.

tag team—when two wrestlers partner together against other teams

17

CHAPTER 3:
MAKING THE BIG TIME

Young Oscar grew up watching Consejo Mundial de Lucha Libre (CMLL) wrestling on TV. This is a Spanish name for the Worldwide Wrestling Council. In the early 1990s some of the key players in that group broke away. They formed a new wrestling promotion company called Asistencia Asesoría y Administración (AAA). The name was Spanish for Assistance, Consulting, and Administration. This organization wanted to highlight big characters like American pro wrestling promotions did. They were looking for new talent.

The AAA focused on young wrestlers such as Rey Mysterio and several of his friends. Joining AAA meant traveling to Mexico City, which was 1,400 miles (2,253 kilometers) from Tijuana. It was a huge change for the young men, but they were excited to be a part of AAA.

In Mexico City, money was tight for Rey and his friends. There were delays in getting the AAA started, and there were no real contracts. At first Rey and the other wrestlers lived in a tiny motel room. They would often pool their money to buy one meal to share. Sometimes Rey wanted to give up, but his family encouraged him to keep trying.

Once the AAA got started, it scheduled matches all over Mexico. As its popularity grew, the matches were televised. The televised matches caught the eyes of pro wrestling promoters in the Unites States. Soon AAA matches were scheduled in Los Angeles, California. Rey Mysterio became a big-time draw for fans—and promoters.

FACT

When they were first in AAA, Rey and his friends ran out of money. For a while, they lived in a gym for free.

Mexico City was more than four times the size of Tijuana. Moving there was a big adjustment for Rey.

THE U.S.A. WRESTLING GAME

In 1995 Rey made the move to pro wrestling in the United States. When he entered U.S. wrestling, there were a few large pro wrestling promotions in play. The smallest was Extreme Championship Wrestling (ECW). Next was World Championship Wrestling (WCW). And the largest company was World Wrestling Federation (WWF), now known as World Wrestling Entertainment (WWE).

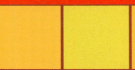

Rey Mysterio signed on with ECW. There he was forced to adjust to a different style of competing. In Mexican wrestling, there were lots of rules about what wrestlers could do. In ECW wrestlers had more freedom to try new moves. Also, U.S. wrestling used **storylines**, which was not common practice in lucha libre. Rey adjusted to the changes and soon caught the attention of WCW officials.

In 1996 Rey began wrestling for WCW. In WCW one of Rey's best friends was Eddie Guerrero. They had both wrestled for AAA. Eddie helped Rey get good matches and interesting storylines. Great storylines made them more popular with fans.

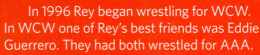

On June 16, 1996, Rey had his first WCW match. He faced Dean Malenko, the Cruiserweight Champion. Malenko knew how to handle Rey's high-flying style. He had faced high-flyers before. Rey was no match for Malenko that first night. But he got another shot at Malenko on July 8, 1996. It was a wild match. At one point Malenko had Rey upside down. But Rey flipped Malenko and pinned him. Suddenly, Rey Mysterio was the new WCW Cruiserweight Champion.

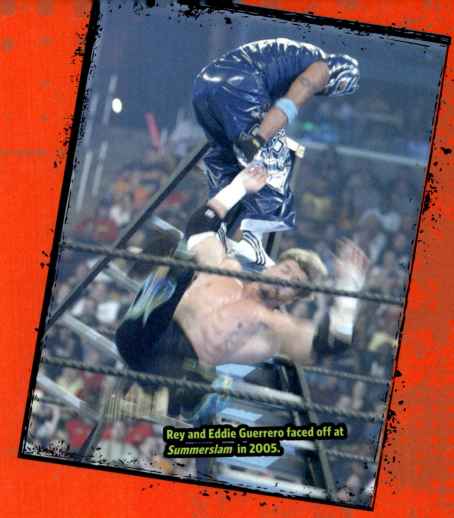

Rey and Eddie Guerrero faced off at *Summerslam* in 2005.

WCW Titles Won

Rey Mysterio had a successful run in WCW. Here are his titles.

Title	Number of Titles Held
WCW Cruiserweight Champion	5
WCW Cruiserweight Tag Team Championship	1 (with Billy Kidman)
WCW World Tag Team Championship	3 (with Konnan, Billy Kidman, and Juventud Guerrera)

storyline—a story that is created for wrestling performances

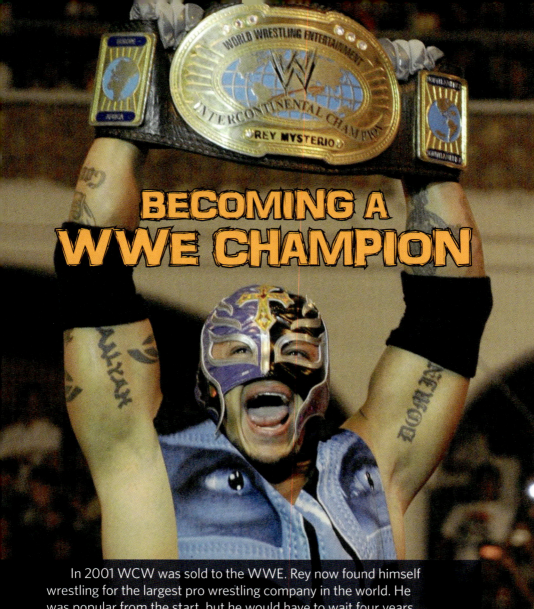

BECOMING A
WWE CHAMPION

In 2001 WCW was sold to the WWE. Rey now found himself wrestling for the largest pro wrestling company in the world. He was popular from the start, but he would have to wait four years before he claimed his first WWE championship.

In 2006 Rey competed in the **ROYAL RUMBLE**. The winner of this match would be given the chance to face Kurt Angle for the WWE Heavyweight Championship title. The Royal Rumble involves 30 wrestlers who compete in order, based on their entry numbers. Rey was the second wrestler, so he had to face 28 other men as they each entered the ring. Rey held strong throughout the marathon match. In the end, it came down to Rey and Randy Orton, and Rey came out on top.

The WWE switched things up, though. Instead of a straight matchup at *WrestleMania* between Rey and Angle, it became a three-way match among Rey, Orton, and Angle. In a match like this, the first person to pin another fighter is the winner. At first, Angle seemed to dominate the match, but Rey did not give up. Eventually, Rey pinned Angle and was declared the WWE Heavyweight Champion.

WHAT DO THOSE TITLES MEAN?

The WWE has many championship titles. They are usually separated between the *Raw* and *SmackDown* brands, which are two different TV programs. Check out the main titles:

- The **World Heavyweight Championship** is the primary title for the *SmackDown* brand but has also been featured on *Raw* in the past. The belt was started in 2002.

- The **WWE Intercontinental Championship** is the secondary title for the *SmackDown* brand. It started in 1979.

- The **WWE Championship** is the primary world title for the *Raw* brand. It was established in 1963.

- The **United States Championship** is the secondary title for the *Raw* brand. It was originally created in 1975 by the National Wrestling Alliance (NWA).

- The **World Cruiserweight Championship** was a professional championship for wrestlers who weighed 220 pounds (100 kg) or less. It was created in 1996 by WCW. The championship was brought into the WWE mix when WCW was purchased. This belt was phased out after 2007.

FACT

Rey has won every one of WWE's five main championships as well as the Tag Team Championship.

CHAPTER 4:
THE LIFE OF A LUCHADOR

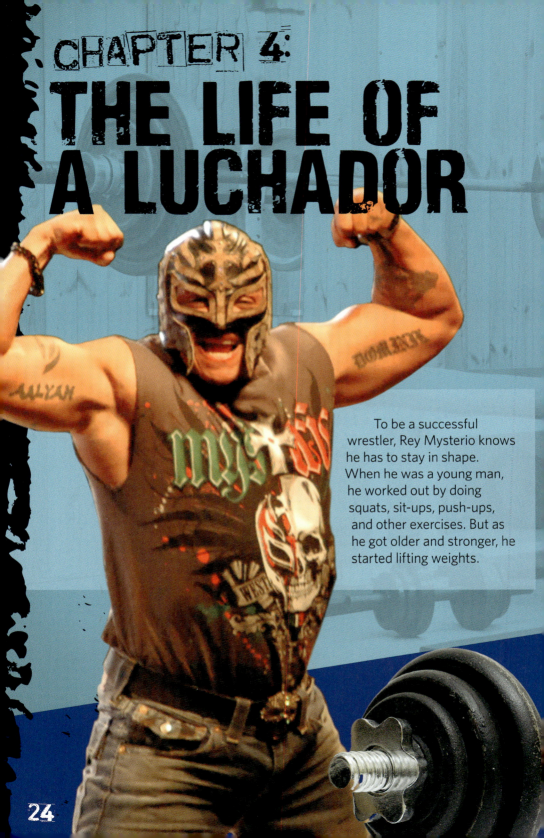

To be a successful wrestler, Rey Mysterio knows he has to stay in shape. When he was a young man, he worked out by doing squats, sit-ups, push-ups, and other exercises. But as he got older and stronger, he started lifting weights.

One very important part of Rey's workout is proper form. Doing a chest press is very precise for him. So are bicep curls and other moves. Nothing is rushed or sloppy.

These days, Rey works out about two hours every day. He does 30 minutes of cardio, which consists of running or working out on an elliptical machine. He spends the rest of his workout time with weights.

Rey knows that diet is an important part of staying in shape too. Protein helps build muscle. Because he is so physically active, he makes sure to get enough protein. Rey often eats egg whites, chicken, and steak, and he drinks protein shakes throughout the day.

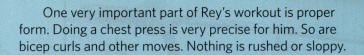

PROTEIN FOOD

Rey admits that sometimes he eats sweets or other treats. But most days, he is careful to eat a healthy, protein-packed diet and get plenty of exercise.

SYMBOLS AND MEANINGS

Rey Mysterio has used his appearance as a way to express himself. Rey is a **Catholic**. He has made his religious beliefs part of his appearance in the ring. His masks often have images of crosses or skulls on them. For people in Mexico, a skull represents life after death. He has a **rosary** tattooed on his chest, as well as several crosses on his body. He also has the phrase "Made man by God" on his wrists.

In addition, Rey has tattoos of his kids' names and an image of him with his wife. He also has his wife's name tattooed on his left ring finger in case he forgets to wear his wedding ring.

On his left shoulder, he has a tattoo of a Japanese character that means "king." On his right shoulder, there is one that means "mystery." Put together, they stand for Rey Mysterio.

BEING UNMASKED

Rey's mask is more than just a part of his costume. Masks are a very important part of the lucha libre tradition. In lucha libre, the mask is part of a wrestler's image and a symbol of respect. In 1999 Rey was pressured by the WCW to let his opponent remove his mask during a match. He was afraid to say no, so he gave in to their request. Rey hated doing it.

Catholic—people who are members of the Catholic Church, the Christian church that is headed by the pope

rosary—a string of beads Catholics use to pray

CHAPTER 5

ALL THE RIGHT MOVES

While Rey was with the WCW, he earned the nickname the Giant Killer. This was because he could take on wrestlers who were much larger than him. Rey used his speed and **agility** to defeat these wrestlers. He could jump from the ropes and over his opponents' heads. He also used his strength and flexibility to flip larger wrestlers. Rey's explosive moves made for exciting matches. Fans eagerly tuned in to watch him take down pro wrestling's giants.

Rey took down Kane in a 2008 matchup.

agility—the ability to move quickly and easily

Some of the "giants" that Rey Mysterio took on included Kane, Scott Norton, Lex Luger, Bam Bam Bigelow, and Kevin Nash. Check out their stats and compare.

WRESTLER	HEIGHT	WEIGHT
Kane	7 feet (213 cm)	323 pounds (147 kg)
Scott Norton	6 feet, 3 inches (191 cm)	360 pounds (163 kg)
Lex Luger	6 feet, 6 inches (198 cm)	275 pounds (125 kg)
Bam Bam Bigelow	6 feet, 4 inches (193 cm)	390 pounds (177 kg)
Kevin Nash	6 feet, 10 inches (208 cm)	328 pounds (149 kg)

REY MYSTERIO

HEIGHT
5 feet, 6 inches (168 cm)

WEIGHT
175 pounds (79 kg)

SIGNATURE MOVES

One way Rey Mysterio keeps his opponents on guard is by having well-rehearsed moves he can rely on. Check out some of the moves he is best known for.

WEST COAST POP

Rey jumps off the top rope and onto his opponent's shoulders. Then he does a backflip, which takes down the other wrestler.

FROG SPLASH

Rey stands on the top rope, jumps off, and stretches out horizontally. Then he pulls his hands and feet in and out before he lands on his opponent.

DROPPIN' DA DIME

This move is named for the practice of using a pay phone (which used to cost a dime). It's a phrase that also means calling the police. For this move, Rey stands outside the ring, leaps over the ropes, and then kicks his opponent.

THE 619

This move is named for Rey's area code in San Diego. He uses it as a **finishing move**. When his opponent is leaning on the ropes, Rey holds on to the top and bottom ropes. He then swings his legs in between them, kicking his opponent.

finishing move—a signature move used to finish off an opponent and end a match

FACT

Rey's finishing move was the inspiration behind a couple of his other nicknames—Master of 619 and Mr. 619.

CHAPTER 6:
FEUDS AND FRIENDSHIPS

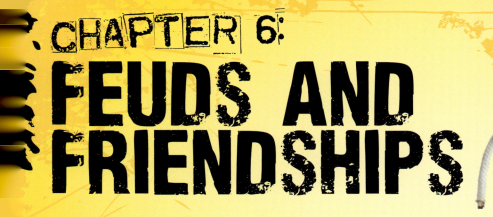

Over the years, Rey Mysterio has faced opponents of many different sizes and backgrounds. He has taunted and teased them, slammed and pinned them—all with memorable style. There's no doubt many of these wrestlers would like to pin Rey Mysterio's picture to a piñata.

CM PUNK

Height: 6 ft, 2 in (188 cm)

Weight: 218 lbs (99 kg)

CM Punk and Rey have battled each other over and over during their careers. They often taunt each other outside the ring.

PSICOSIS

Height: 5 ft, 10 in (178 cm)

Weight: 200 lbs (91 kg)

Psicosis lost to Rey in a 2006 Royal Rumble match.

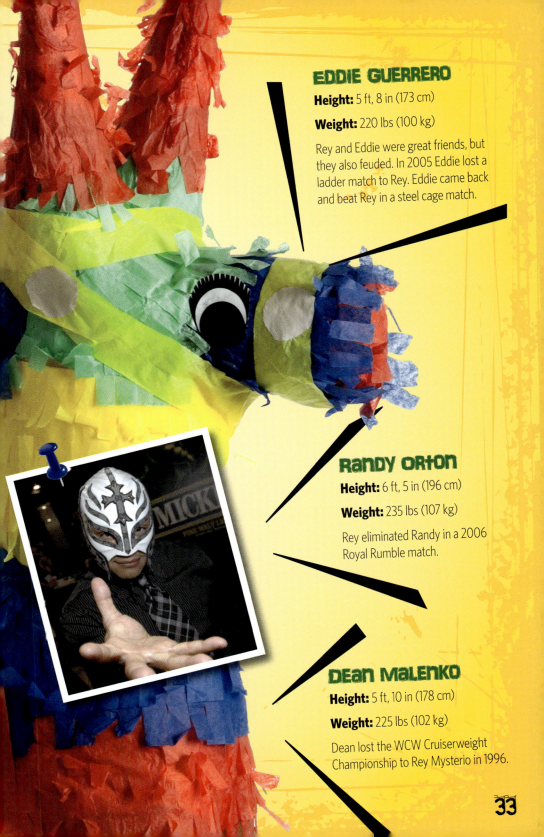

EDDIE GUERRERO

Height: 5 ft, 8 in (173 cm)

Weight: 220 lbs (100 kg)

Rey and Eddie were great friends, but they also feuded. In 2005 Eddie lost a ladder match to Rey. Eddie came back and beat Rey in a steel cage match.

RANDY ORTON

Height: 6 ft, 5 in (196 cm)

Weight: 235 lbs (107 kg)

Rey eliminated Randy in a 2006 Royal Rumble match.

DEAN MALENKO

Height: 5 ft, 10 in (178 cm)

Weight: 225 lbs (102 kg)

Dean lost the WCW Cruiserweight Championship to Rey Mysterio in 1996.

TAGGING UP

Rey Mysterio has proven his value as an individual wrestler. But he can be even more entertaining when he teams up with other wrestlers. Rey has had great success as part of tag teams. Check out a couple of his most notable partners.

FILTHY ANIMALS

The Filthy Animals were a WCW **stable** that included Rey Mysterio, Konnan, Billy Kidman, and Eddie Guerrero. Together they wreaked havoc from 1999 to 2001. Whether the Filthy Animals were playing babyfaces or heels, fans loved their antics. Rey Mysterio won the WCW World Tag Team Championship with Konnan and Billy Kidman. He also won the WCW Cruiserweight Tag Team Championship with Billy Kidman. Rey's time with the Filthy Animals was one of the few periods during which he wrestled without a mask.

KONNAN'S STATS

HEIGHT
5 ft, 11 in (180 cm)

WEIGHT
250 lbs (113 kg)

SIGNATURE MOVE
Tequila Sunrise

BILLY KIDMAN'S STATS

HEIGHT
5 ft, 10 in (178 cm)

WEIGHT
195 lbs (88 kg)

SIGNATURE MOVE
Shooting Star Press

EDDIE GUERRERO'S STATS

HEIGHT
5 ft, 8 in (173 cm)

WEIGHT
220 lbs (100 kg)

SIGNATURE MOVE
Frog Splash

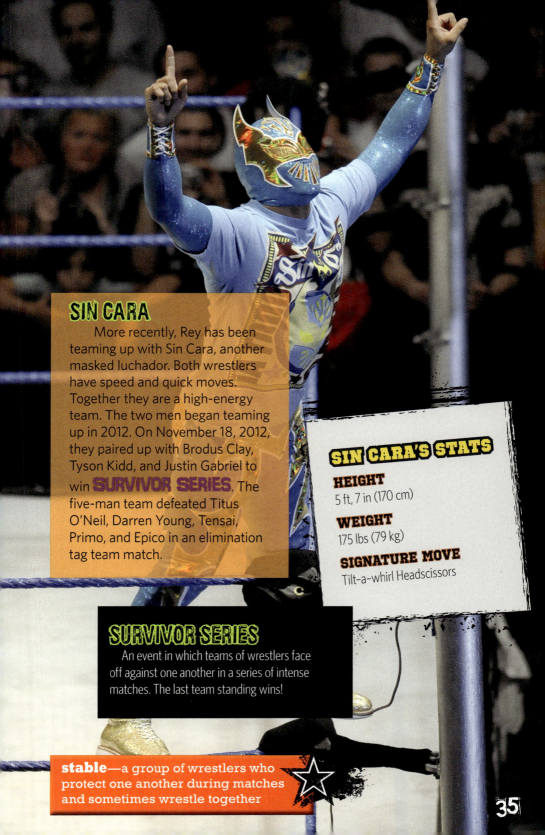

SIN CARA

More recently, Rey has been teaming up with Sin Cara, another masked luchador. Both wrestlers have speed and quick moves. Together they are a high-energy team. The two men began teaming up in 2012. On November 18, 2012, they paired up with Brodus Clay, Tyson Kidd, and Justin Gabriel to win **SURVIVOR SERIES**. The five-man team defeated Titus O'Neil, Darren Young, Tensai, Primo, and Epico in an elimination tag team match.

SIN CARA'S STATS

HEIGHT
5 ft, 7 in (170 cm)

WEIGHT
175 lbs (79 kg)

SIGNATURE MOVE
Tilt-a-whirl Headscissors

SURVIVOR SERIES

An event in which teams of wrestlers face off against one another in a series of intense matches. The last team standing wins!

stable—a group of wrestlers who protect one another during matches and sometimes wrestle together

KEEPING EDDIE'S MEMORY ALIVE

In some matchups Rey and Eddie Guerrero may have been feuding, but outside the ring they could always rely on each other. The two men trained together, and Guerrero always looked out for Rey. Sadly, Eddie Guerrero died of a heart attack in 2005. He was only 38 years old. Rey was overcome with grief after losing his friend.

FEUDING WITH CHAVO

After Eddie died, Rey wanted his wrestling to serve as a tribute to his old friend. But Eddie's nephew Chavo Guerrero did not agree with that plan. Chavo was also a wrestler, and he felt *he* should be the one to carry on Eddie's memory. This argument led to Rey and Chavo feuding with each other for a number of years.

Even when they weren't wrestling against each other, they tried to bring each other down. In the *Great American Bash* in 2006, Rey was competing against King Booker, but Chavo interfered. He ran into the ring and grabbed a chair, looking like he was going to attack Booker. Instead, he slammed it against Rey's head, and Booker won the match.

Rey and Eddie Guerrero faced each other at *WrestleMania* in 2005.

CHAPTER 7: FALLING HARD

No matter how well-trained they are, pro wrestlers face many bumps, bruises, and breaks. Rey Mysterio is no exception. In fact, his high-flying style of wrestling probably makes him more likely to suffer injuries.

ACL TEAR

In 1997 Rey tore the anterior cruciate ligament (ACL) in his right knee. The ACL is an important tissue that holds the knee joint together. Rey underwent surgery that used other human tissue to repair the ACL. After a few months of **rehabilitation**, he was back in the ring.

ACL REPAIR

A few months after his return, Rey knew his knee wasn't feeling right. As it turned out, his body had rejected the tissue from the earlier operation. He had another operation and went through more rehabilitation.

ACL RUPTURE

In 2006 Rey experienced another ACL issue, this time in his left knee. He had an operation to repair his ACL and a **tendon** in his knee. He spent several months building his strength back up.

rehabilitation—therapy that helps people recover their health or abilities

ARTHROSCOPIC SURGERY

Years later, Rey felt pain in his left knee again and had to have **arthroscopic** surgery to repair it. In the years since, his knees continue to give him trouble.

BICEP TEAR

In 2008 Rey was in a match when he tore his bicep, a big muscle in his upper arm. This led to surgery, but the wound would not heal. He had another surgery, and another, and then several months of rehabilitation.

tendon—a strong band of tissue that attaches muscles to bones

arthroscopic—describing surgery that is performed with the help of a long tube called an arthroscope

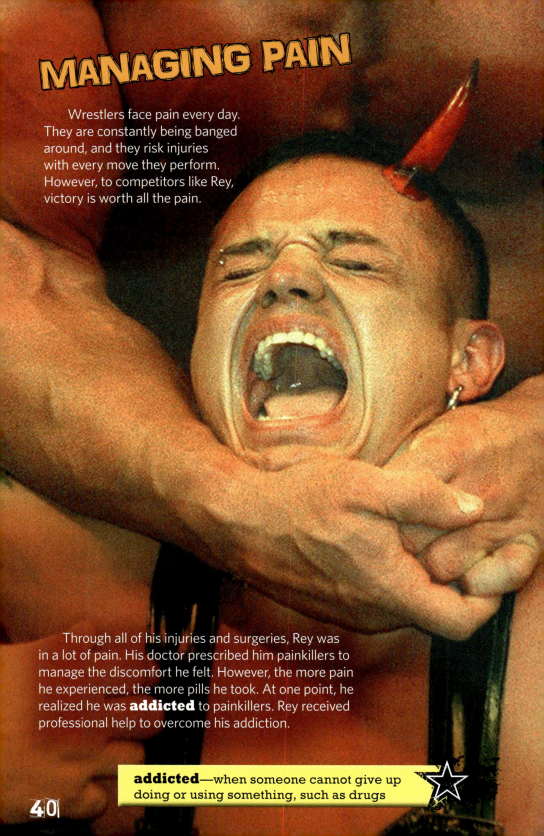

MANAGING PAIN

Wrestlers face pain every day. They are constantly being banged around, and they risk injuries with every move they perform. However, to competitors like Rey, victory is worth all the pain.

Through all of his injuries and surgeries, Rey was in a lot of pain. His doctor prescribed him painkillers to manage the discomfort he felt. However, the more pain he experienced, the more pills he took. At one point, he realized he was **addicted** to painkillers. Rey received professional help to overcome his addiction.

addicted—when someone cannot give up doing or using something, such as drugs

STRAIGHT DOPE

When it comes to **steroid** use, Rey knows it is not the way to go. Some people accused him of taking these drugs, but he states he has never touched them. He hopes his young fans will steer clear of them too.

"Wrestling is a constant challenge. You push your body every night. It hurts—it hurts beyond words. But the mind wants to soar, and the body must follow. I love it."
—Rey Mysterio on wrestling through the pain
(Rey Mysterio: Behind the Mask)

In 2012 Rey failed a WWE drug test. This means that drugs that the WWE does not approve of were found in his body. Rey claimed he did not know what they were. Officials stated they might have been medications Rey was taking to lose weight. No matter where they came from, Rey knows he should have been more careful. He was not allowed to wrestle for two months.

steroid—a drug used by athletes to improve their performance

CHAPTER 8:
OUTSIDE THE RING

There's more to Rey Mysterio than a masked man in the wrestling ring. When he's not wrestling, Rey loves to spend time with his family.

When young Oscar was training at the gym in Tijuana, he met a girl named Angie. For him, it was love at first sight. On May 11, 1996, Rey Mysterio and Angie were married.

1996

1997

On April 5, 1997, Angie gave birth to a son, Dominik. Rey injured his knee soon after Dominik was born. Rey was unhappy to be hurt, but very glad to spend his time healing at home with his new baby.

"I was very fortunate to have been there for the birth of both my son and my daughter, and to get the chance to spend time with them when they were very little."
—Rey Mysterio
(Rey Mysterio: Behind the Mask)

FACT

Rey Mysterio and his family live in San Diego.

On August 20, 2001, Angie and Rey welcomed a daughter named Aalyah. The WCW had just been bought by the WWE. It was a confusing time. But it meant that Rey finished up his WCW contract at home and could spend time with his new daughter.

2001

INSPIRING HIS FANS

Rey Mysterio is a role model for kids all over the world. He treats other wrestlers with respect, and he follows the rules. Young fans can admire the way Rey acts and carries himself.

Rey visits elementary schools and talks to kids about standing up against bullying.

Rey is careful to take good care of his body through healthy nutrition and exercise. He advises young athletes to learn what's best for their individual bodies. He also says it's important to stretch and warm up before every workout.

ENTERTAINING THE TROOPS

In December 2008, Rey Mysterio made his third visit to Iraq to visit U.S. troops. He also traveled there in 2004 and 2007. Rey enjoys putting on a show for the military men and women, and he considers these shows some of the high points of his career.

"I've been humbled by the reaction of the men and women I've met every time ...They're all so grateful for us coming out. But really, we're the ones who are grateful. They put their lives on the line for us, for our freedom, for our children. They're real heroes." **—Rey Mysterio on entertaining the troops**
(Rey Mysterio: Behind the Mask)

Rey's injuries may slow him down a bit. But with his passion and determination, there's no telling how far his pro wrestling dreams will take him.

GLOSSARY

addicted (uh-DIK-tud)—when someone cannot give up doing or using something, such as drugs

agility (uh-JIL-uh-tee)—the ability to move quickly and easily

arthroscopic (ar-thruh-SKAH-pik)—describes a surgery that is performed with the help of a long tube called an arthroscope

babyface (BAY-bee-fayss)—a wrestler who acts as a hero in the ring

Catholic (KATH-uh-lik)—people who are members of the Catholic Church, the Christian church that is headed by the pope

finishing move (FIN-ish-ing MOOV)—a signature move used to finish off an opponent and end a match

heel (HEEL)—a wrestler who acts as a villain in the ring

luchador (LOO-chah-dor)—a term for a professional wrestler in Mexico

rehabilitation (ree-huh-bil-uh-TAY-shun)—therapy that helps people recover their health or abilities

rosary (ROH-zuh-ree)—a string of beads used for prayer in the Catholic religion

stable (STAY-buhl)—a group of wrestlers who protect one another during matches and sometimes wrestle together

steroid (STIHR-oid)—a drug used by athletes to improve their performance

storyline (STOR-ee-lyne)—a story that is created about feuds and friendships for wrestling performances

tag team (TAG TEEM)—when two wrestlers partner together against other teams

tendon (TEN-duhn)—a strong band of tissue that attaches muscles to bones

READ MORE

Kaelberer, Angie Peterson. *The Fabulous, Freaky, Unusual History of Pro Wrestling.* Unusual Histories. Mankato, Minn.: Capstone Press, 2011.

Sullivan, Kevin. *Rey Mysterio.* DK Readers. New York: DK Pub., 2011.

West, Tracey. *Rey Mysterio: Giant Slayer.* New York: Grosset & Dunlap, 2011.

INTERNET SITES

FactHound offers a safe, fun way to find Internet sites related to this book. All of the sites on FactHound have been researched by our staff.

Here's all you do:

Visit *www.facthound.com*

Enter this code: 9781429699730

INDEX